TODAY I THOUGHT I'D RUN AWAY

JANE JOHNSON

E. P. DUTTON   NEW YORK

Library of Congress Cataloging in Publication Data

Johnson, Jane, date
  Today I thought I'd run away.

  Summary: When he decides to run away, a young
boy packs a bag with special things that help
protect him from the ogre, goblin, dragon, and
other monsters that he meets on the way.
  1. Children's stories, English.
[1. Monsters—Fiction] I. Title.
PZ7.J63216To 1985 [E] 84-25920
ISBN 0-525-44193-X

Published in the United States by E. P. Dutton, Inc.,
2 Park Avenue, New York, N.Y. 10016
Printed in Great Britain by Hazell Watson & Viney Ltd.,
member of the BPCC Group, Aylesbury, Bucks.
First Edition   OBE   10 9 8 7 6 5 4 3 2 1

Today I thought I'd run away.
So I went upstairs
and got my bag

and packed it
with my special things,

and set out.

I hadn't gone very far when I met
a grumbling, rumbling, lumbering ogre.
So I opened my bag and took out
my comb and threw it on
the ground . . .

and made a forest grow. It was too thick for
the ogre, but I ran through it and left him behind.

I hadn't gone very far when I met
a wriggling, giggling, grinning
goblin.

So I opened
my bag and took out
my egg-cup and threw it
on the ground . . .

and made a mountain rise.
It was too high for the goblin,

but I climbed over it and left him behind.

I hadn't gone very far when I met

a hissing, spitting, sizzling dragon.
So I opened my bag
and took out my belt

and threw it on the ground . . .

and made a river flow.

It was too wet for the dragon,
but I swam across it and left him behind.

I hadn't gone very far when I met
a whirling, twirling, swirling demon.

So I opened my bag and took out my scarf

and threw it on the ground . . .

and made a blizzard blow.
It was too cold for the demon,
but I got through it and left him behind.

I hadn't gone very far when I met

a howling, growling, yowling monster.
So I opened my bag and took out
dad's old hat and rammed it
on my head . . .

and marched up closer to the monster
(but not too close).

"Behave yourself!" I said
in my loudest voice.

And he did.

I picked up my bag to go on, but it was empty.

So I went home
to find more things
to put in it.

It was late when I got back.
So I think I'll run away again . . .

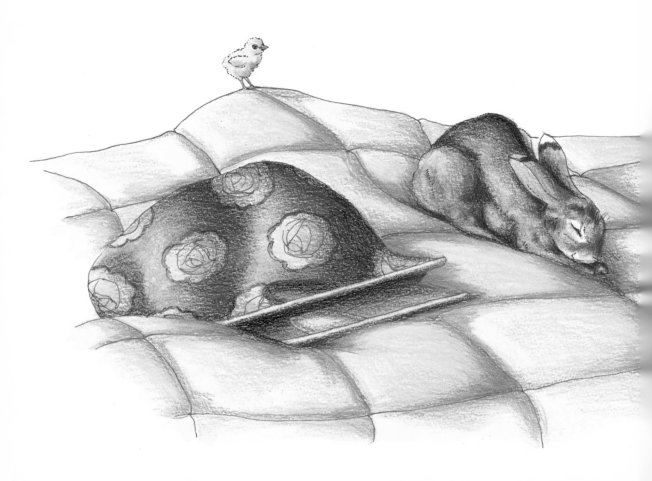

tomorrow.

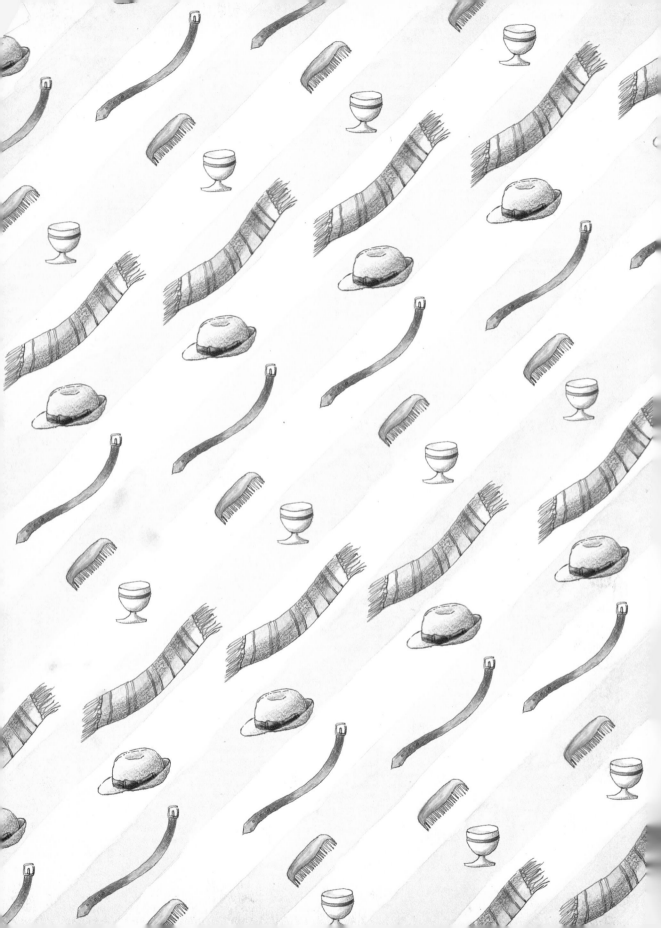